Honeypot Hill

Saffron Thimble's
Sewing Shop

To the City

The Orchards

Paddle Steamer
Quay

Aunt
Marigold'
General
Store

Lavender Valley
Garden Centre

Healing House and Garden

The Worthingtons' House

Melody
Maker's
Music Shop

Lavender Lake

Bumble Bee's Teashop

Lavender Lake
School of Dance

Peppermint
Pond

Hedgerows Hotel
Where Mimosa lives

SCHOOL

Rosehip School

Summer Meadow

Christmas Corner

Wildspice Woods

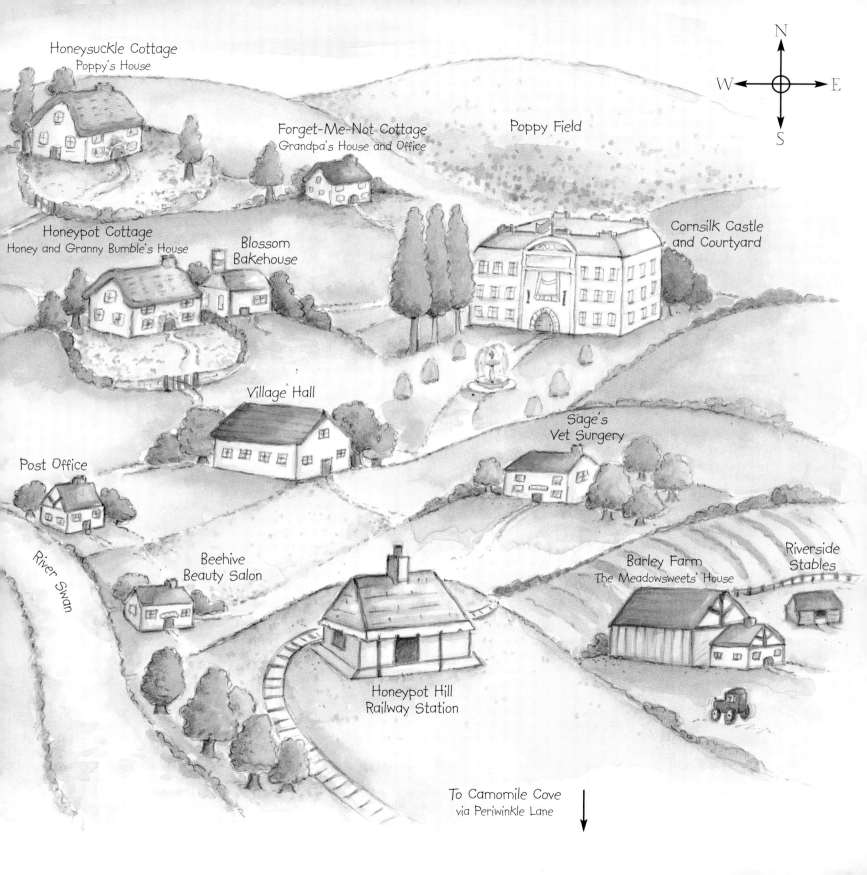

Honeysuckle Cottage
Poppy's House

Forget-Me-Not Cottage
Grandpa's House and Office

Poppy Field

N
W ——⊕—— E
S

Honeypot Cottage
Honey and Granny Bumble's House

Blossom
Bakehouse

Cornsilk Castle
and Courtyard

Village Hall

Sage's
Vet Surgery

Post Office

River Swan

Beehive
Beauty Salon

Barley Farm
The Meadowsweets' House

Riverside
Stables

Honeypot Hill
Railway Station

To Camomile Cove
via Periwinkle Lane

Check out Princess Poppy's brilliant website:

www.princesspoppy.com

MERMAID PRINCESS
A PICTURE CORGI BOOK 978 0 552 55923 2

First published in Great Britain by Picture Corgi,
an imprint of Random House Children's Books
A Random House Group Company

This edition published 2009

1 3 5 7 9 10 8 6 4 2

Text copyright © Janey Louise Jones, 2009
Illustration copyright © Picture Corgi Books, 2009
Illustrations by Veronica Vasylenko
Design by Tracey Cunnell

Picture Corgi Books are published by Random House Children's Books,
61–63 Uxbridge Road, London W5 5SA

www.kidsatrandomhouse.co.uk
www.princesspoppy.com

Addresses for companies within The Random House Group Limited
can be found at: www.randomhouse.co.uk/offices.htm

THE RANDOM HOUSE GROUP Limited Reg. No. 954009

A CIP catalogue record for this book is available from the British Library.

Printed in China

Mermaid Princess

Written by Janey Louise Jones

PICTURE CORGI

For Evelyn, Julie and Lilian,
my special friends,
with love

Mermaid Princess

featuring

Honey
★

Daisy
★

Edward
★

Princess Poppy

Flora
★

Mum
★

Dad
★

"Hurrah! I love carnival day!"
Poppy cried as the train chuffed into
Camomile Cove station.

"Me too!" replied Honey. "I really
hope one of us will be crowned
Mermaid Princess this year!"

As soon as the train stopped at the platform, Poppy and Honey jumped down and started making their way towards Shellbay House, where Poppy's cousin, Daisy lived.

They couldn't wait to put on their carnival costumes and join the parade.

"Hang on, girls," called Mum as the grown-ups tried to organize the twins and all the picnic baskets and buckets and spades, but Poppy and Honey were already halfway up the road.

"Hi, Daisy!" said Poppy as they saw her older cousin waving from the doorway of her summer house. "Wow! Your costume is amazing."

Daisy was already dressed up in her mermaid outfit, all ready for the carnival, so she helped the other two girls to get changed into theirs.

Then she styled their hair
and added a few accessories.

"I'm sure one of you two will win the Mermaid Princess crown this year!" exclaimed Daisy when Poppy and Honey's outfits were complete.

They were sparkling with sequins, beads and pearly shells and they both looked wonderful.

Just then Daisy's younger brother, Edward, burst through the door.

"Come on, you lot. We have to leave for the parade, or Mum says we'll all be late," he said.

The happy group hurried to the clock tower, where the children's parade was about to begin. Poppy, Honey, Daisy and Edward waved goodbye to the grown-ups and the twins and set off round the town with all the other children.

The parade was amazing to look at with so many wonderful costumes – although Poppy secretly thought hers was the best – and lots of brightly coloured streamers and balloons. They were so excited to be part of it.

Just then, among all the noise and people, Poppy noticed a girl standing all alone.

"Are you all right?" called Poppy as she pushed through the parade towards her.

"No!" sobbed the little girl miserably. "My tiara has been knocked off and now it's broken so my costume is spoiled *and* I've lost my friends."

"Oh, poor you!" said Poppy. "I'm Poppy. What's your name?"

"It's Flora Jane Tomkins," replied the girl, between sniffs and sobs.

"Why don't you come with me and my friends?" suggested Poppy.
"We'll help you find your friends after the parade."

"Yes please," replied Flora, smiling through her tears.

Then Poppy did something very unusual . . .

"Oh, and why don't you have this?" said Poppy, taking off her tiara and offering it to Flora. "I've got so many sparkly things on my costume that I don't really need it anyway."

"Are you sure?" asked Flora as she took the tiara and put it on.

"Um, yes," said Poppy, pleased that she had made Flora feel better but a little sad about giving away her gorgeous tiara.

"Thank you!" smiled Flora.

"Come on, Poppy!" called Daisy, suddenly noticing that her cousin had dropped behind. "The costume competition is in five minutes."

"Coming," replied Poppy as she grabbed Flora's hand and made her way towards the others.

As the parade came to a stop, Daisy looked at Poppy's bare head, then at Flora's tiara, but before she could ask what had happened, an announcement started booming through the loud speakers.

"To find out who will be crowned this year's Mermaid Princess and Lord of the Sea, can all those contestants wishing to take part in the costume competition please make their way to the harbour wall immediately?"

Poppy, Daisy, Honey, Edward and Flora stood by the harbour wall together, all dizzy with nerves and excitement. Each of them was absolutely desperate to win!

The boy's prize was announced first and the girls went wild when
Edward's name was called. They giggled as he hopped onto the platform
on one leg and was crowned Lord of the Sea.

All the mermaids in the crowd began to tremble as the special coral crown of the Mermaid Princess was taken from the prize box. Poppy held her breath.

"This year, we are awarding the Mermaid Princess prize to a very special girl. She has a wonderful costume but there was something else we noticed during the parade, something more important than her costume.

She knows what I'm talking about. So I am delighted to announce that this year, the Mermaid Princess prize goes to . . .

"Miss Poppy Cotton. Come up to the stage please, Princess Poppy!"
Poppy felt as if she was dreaming. Daisy proudly led her onto
the stage. Mum waved up at her, while Dad took photographs.

Poppy smiled as the judge put the magnificent coral crown on her head.

"Now, to complete the carnival parade the Mermaid Princess and the Lord of the Sea will ride through the streets in a horse-drawn carriage," said the judge as the crowd clapped and cheered.

All of Poppy's friends and family, including Flora, who had now been reunited with her own group, followed the carriage, cheering all the way. Dad jogged to keep up so that he could take photos.

"You're a perfect Mermaid Princess, Poppy," said Dad when the carriage came to a stop. "The kindest princess – which is why you deserve your coral crown!"

Poppy smiled – it had been the best carnival ever!